In a corner of Moat Farm stood an old barn. It was dark in the barn and Farmer Green stored lots of things there, like old horse-carts, tools, and bits of wood. Some of these things had been stored there for so long that Farmer Green had forgotten all about them.

On one side of the barn was an old red tractor. It was a little bit rusty and there were cobwebs hanging down from it. Apart from Molly and Tolly, who often slept there, no one came in the barn much.

One evening, the big green tractor had broken down. Farmer Green was in the yard, mending it. He stood up and scratched his head under his cap.

"It is too late to go and get the part I need," he said to himself. "It will have to wait until morning."

Just then, he happened to look up at the barn.

“Hmm,” he said, thinking. “Perhaps, in the barn, there is an old part that I can use to mend the tractor. If there is, I can finish my jobs off this evening, instead of waiting. I need this big tractor to help with the harvest as I can attach the big grain-trailer to it.”

Farmer Green went to the barn and looked into the gloom.

In the barn, he found himself standing next to the old red tractor. He looked at it and rubbed its paint.

"You were a good old thing," he said, patting it fondly. "I had forgotten you were in here. Still, I suppose I must get on."

He went back to looking for the part he needed to mend the big green tractor. He bent down and picked up some bits of metal from the ground.

“No, no,” he muttered, and shook his head. Then he found something under some wood. “That looks more like it!” he said, but when he looked at it properly, he said, “No, this is no good. I need something bigger.”

Next, Farmer Green looked around at the back of the barn.

"This looks more promising," he said, as he found a box crammed with old odds and ends. "Yes! Perfect!" he exclaimed, as he stood up. "This will do the job," and off he set to finish mending the big green tractor.

Just as he was about to go outside, Farmer Green stopped and looked back at the old red tractor.

"Hmm!" he said, rubbing his chin. "I need a small tractor to help me. And all this one needs is some oil and a good brush-down."

Next morning, he came back to start mending the old red tractor. He took it out of the barn and into the yard, where it stood looking dusty and battered.

Farmer Green brushed off all the cobwebs and dust. Then he fetched his hose and scrubbed the tractor down.

He spent the whole weekend mending the tractor.

"Well," said Sally, his wife, when he had finished, "the tractor looks better. Let's see if she drives better, too."

Farmer Green clambered up into the tractor.

"Fingers crossed!" he called.

The tractor roared into life, and there was a big cloud of smoke. Ben and Neb woke up and started barking loudly. Molly, Tolly, and the hens all ran to hide. Farmer Green took the brake off and started to drive the old red tractor around the yard.

When he got back to Sally, she clapped.

“There is going to be an old tractor rally next weekend,” she said. “What about entering this old red tractor for it?”

“Perhaps,” nodded Farmer Green. “The paint is still a bit chipped but I suppose I can do something about that.”

“Yes,” said Sally, “and I can help.”

The morning of the rally was hot. Sally had polished the paint on the old red tractor so that it shone in the sunshine. She and Farmer Green drove it to where the rally was going to start.

There were all sorts of old tractors there, lined up along the side of the road. Farmer Green and Sally parked at the end of the line and went to collect a flag and a card with a number on it.

They tied the card onto the tractor and fixed on the flag. By the time the rally was due to start, there were about twenty tractors waiting to go. At the signal, they all started up.

They drove until lunch time, when all the tractors stopped and parked. They had a big picnic. Then everyone drove on to the finish line.

When Sally and Farmer Green arrived home that evening, they were worn out but happy. They parked the old red tractor back in the barn, and Sally gave it a quick polish to wipe off the dust from the road.

"I'm so glad you mended this tractor," she said. "I had a very good time."

Farmer Green patted the tractor and smiled.

"Yes, so did I," he said, looking proudly at the prize in his hand. Not only had the old red tractor finished the whole rally, but it had got a prize for being the best-polished tractor of all!